DING DONG DING DONG

Margie Palatini

Illustrated by Howard Fine

Hyperion Books for Children/New York

Printed in Hong Kong by South China Printing Company Ltd.

First Edition

1 3 5 7 9 10 8 6 4 2

The artwork for each picture is prepared using pastels.
This book is set in 17-point BeLucian.

Library of Congress Cataloging-in-Publication Data

Palatini, Margie.

Ding dong, ding dong/Margie Palatini; illustrated by Howard Fine.—1st edition.

p. cm.

Summary: Despite repeated difficulties, a large ape tries various approaches to
selling Ape-On Cosmetics and his persistence pays off in an unexpected way.

ISBN 0-7868-0420-3 (tr.)—ISBN 0-7868-2367-4 (lib.)

[1. Apes—Fiction. 2. Selling—Fiction. 3. New York (N. Y.)—Fiction.

4. Humorous Stories.] I. Fine, Howard, ill. II. Title.

PZ7.P1755Di 1999

[E]—dc21 98–39548

For my brother
—*M. P.*

For Bill and Jeanne,
wonderful parents and grandparents
—*H. F.*

"Go away! Don't need any."

"Go away! Don't want any."

DING DONG DING DONG

Slam! Bam! "SCRAM, you big ape!"

"EEEE-OOOOOOOOOOOW!"

Oh, wow. Being a door-to-door salesman for Ape-On Cosmetics was no easy job.

No matter how hard he tried, the Big Guy just couldn't get his foot in the door.

"It's a jungle out there!" he moaned as he rubbed his stubbed tootsies. Even though he'd graduated at the top of his class with a degree in Monkey Business, the Big Boy just couldn't get ahead. He hadn't been able to make one single, simple sale.

Not a spritz of Gorilla My Dreams. Not even a smudge of Ape-ricot Lip Gloss. A powdery puff of No More Monkey Shine? He couldn't give the stuff away.

"What am I doing wrong?" he wondered. "I'm one big appealing guy . . . I don't get it."

But the Big Galoot wouldn't give up. He just knew he was bound for success. So he studied harder.

"Let's see," he said, flipping the pages of his *How to Sell Anything, Anywhere, to Anybody—Without Even Trying* sales manual.

"Chapter 1: Location. Location. Location."

Location?

Hey, this chimp was no chump. He wasn't going to let his career wilt on the vine. Uh-uh. No more monkeying around.

He picked up, packed up, and headed out.

The Big City. Gotham. Metropolis. Big Apple. Yes, sir. That was the place for him all right. And he was ready to take a bite.

He pounded the pavement. East Side. West Side. All around the town. He looked the Bronx up and the Battery down.

BEEP! BEEP! BEEP! BEEP!

"MOVE IT, BUB!"

HONK! HONK!

"YOU'RE BLOCKING TRAFFIC, YOU BIG APE!"

BEEP! BEEP! BEEP!

"GET GOING, YOU GRIDLOCKING LUMMOX!"

"Now, I'm in a real jam!" he muttered between the cramming and the crunch.

It was back to the book.

"Chapter 2," he read aloud. "Think Big."

So he thought big. Really BIG.

With his Ape-On beauty case in *toe*, and determined more than ever to make it to the top, the Big Guy set his sights high.

He looked up. Up. Up. Waaay up.

All those windows. All those doors . . .

"If I can make it here, I can make it anywhere," he sang out with confidence.

He slicked back his hair. Made sure his breath was minty fresh. He was ready

to ring the bell!

"Get to work!" said a man coming through the revolving door.

"Work? Yes, sir! Yes, sir!"

Pssst. Pssst. "Gorilla Mist?" he stammered, offering a bit of spray.

"Mist. Water. Whatever." The man handed over a bucket. "Just clean the windows. And make it snappy."

"A window washer?" The Big Fella frowned. "But I don't do windows . . . do I?"

He turned to Chapter 3. "Get In—and Clean Up."

Clean up?

"I'll do it!" he roared, grabbing the bucket and sopping up soapsuds. "I'll work my way to the top if it's the last thing I do!"

And so the Big Guy . . . with his book . . . and his case of Ape-On Cosmetics . . . and a pail of soapy water . . . squeegeed his way up the building. There just had to be a sale up there somewhere. Somehow. With someone. And he was going to find it!

By the seventy-ninth floor the Big Boy had washed 395 windows. And that was only on the south side of the building. However, he still hadn't sold even one tube of Orangutan Cheek Blush. He was beginning to wonder if selling was up his tree.

But then. *Then.*

On the 81st floor, through a half-open window he had just squeegeed squeaky-clean, he saw . . . her. She was lovely. A beauty.

Ch–ching$ Ch–ching$ Ch–ching$ . . . A sure sale!

This was it! His big chance! The Hairy Hunk flashed his big pearly whites and showed some of that ol' chest-pounding personality.

"Aa-a-a-a-ah!
Aa-a-a-ah!

. . . ah, Madam?"

"May I interest you in some of our lovely Ape-On beauty products?" he asked, swinging into action.

"This shade of ape-ricot is absolutely you! Perhaps a whiff of our fragrant 'Da-Vine' jungle perfume? Drives 'em wild. Or how about our two-for-one special? An appealing Banana Cream Facial and our vitamin-packed Monkey C, Monkey Dew Lotion."

The woman smiled.

Oh, boy! Oh, boy! He had her right in the palm of his hand. He was on the edge of a giant sale!

He was just about to spray her a spritz and sniff the sweet smell of success,
when, wouldn't you know it, his big toe slipped!

"Oooooooooh! Oooooooooh! Oooooooooh!"

The Big Fella looked down. Big mistake.

He got dizzy.

Very dizzy.

Very very dizzy.

His ears buzzed. His eyes crossed. His knees buckled.

Before his toe could grab hold, the Big Guy . . . and his book
. . . and his case of Ape-On Cosmetics were taking a tumble.

"Oh-Oh-OooooooooooooooooOH!"

"This beauty business is back-breaking," he moaned, stopping traffic. "I just gotta find another line of work."

"Don't move a muscle!" a gent cried out from the crowd. "That face! That body! That . . . that . . . that look!"

"Huh?"

"And you can act, too! What a delivery! Now what's a tall, dark, and handsome guy like you doing in the street? A monster talent like yourself belongs in Hollywood, fella."

"Huh?"

"The movies need strong silent types. You're a natural! Believe me kid, you can be a star! A BIG star. A box office KING! Sign here on the dotted line."

So . . .

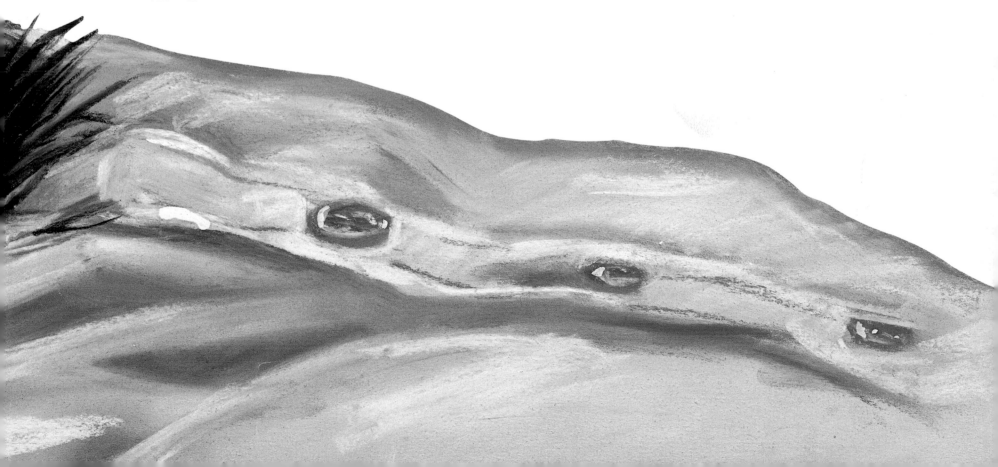

. . . the Big Guy signed. Dealed. And delivered. (His lines, that is.)
And the rest, as they say . . . is history.

"Have your people call my people. We'll do lunch."